Chirri and Chirra are having afternoon tea
when they hear something loud
from the pantry downstairs.

There's a hole in the wall
and something is scurrying inside!

Chirri and Chirra hop on their bicycles and follow along.

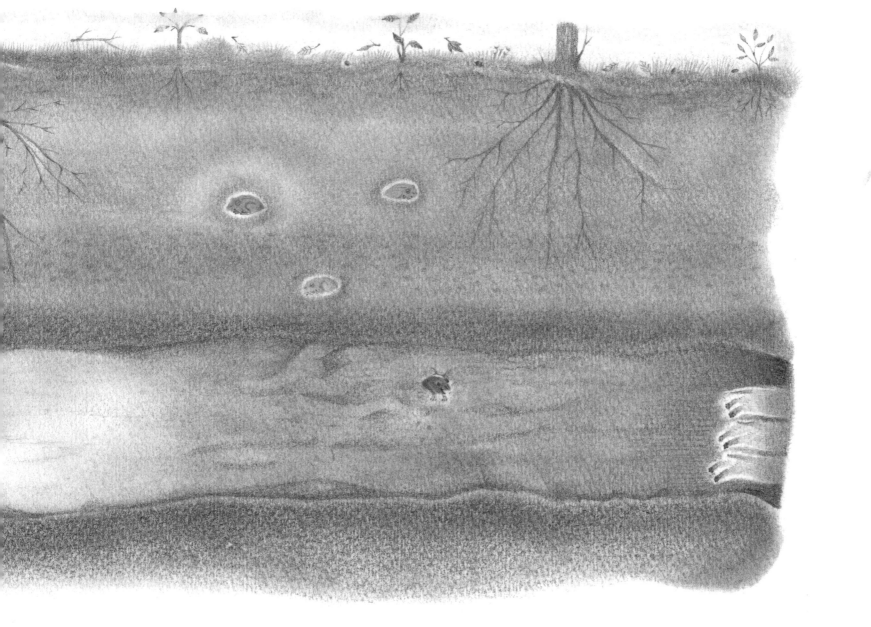

Dring–dring, dring–dring!
Which way did they go?

Chirri and Chirra follow a tunnel of roots
until they see a golden light.

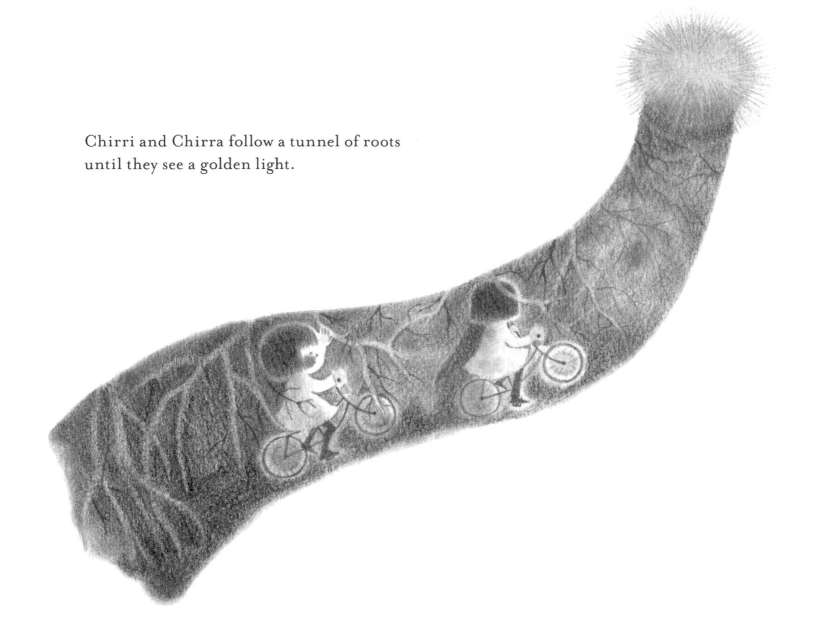

It's an underground peanut farm
and everyone is helping
in a different way.

For you.

Two cones of peanut soft-serve,
warm and fresh as can be.

Dring-dring, dring-dring!
Next, they follow a very narrow tunnel
until they see a rainbow-colored light.

It's an underground flower garden
with flowers of all colors and shapes.

A pair of mayflies comes to greet them.

The mayflies bring flower hats in just the right size.

Dring-dring, dring-dring!
The next tunnel brings them under a vegetable garden.

Ah! There they are again.
Chirri and Chirra pedal after them.

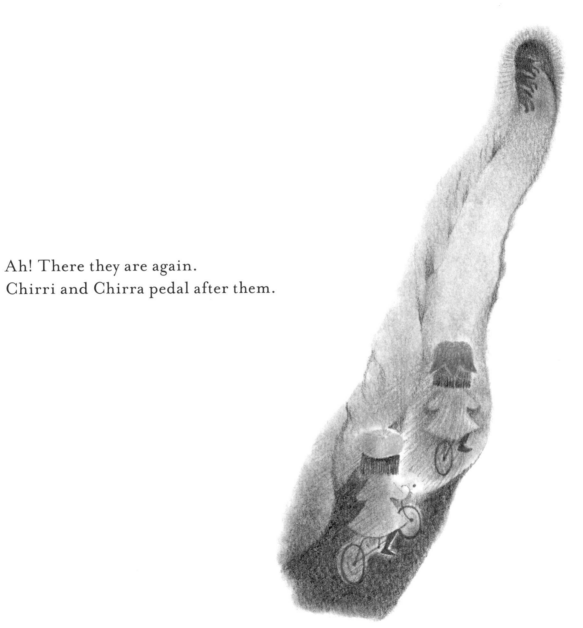

It's a family of badgers!
"Our children went out for apples,
but they took a wrong turn
and broke through your wall …

… We'd like to make it up to you."

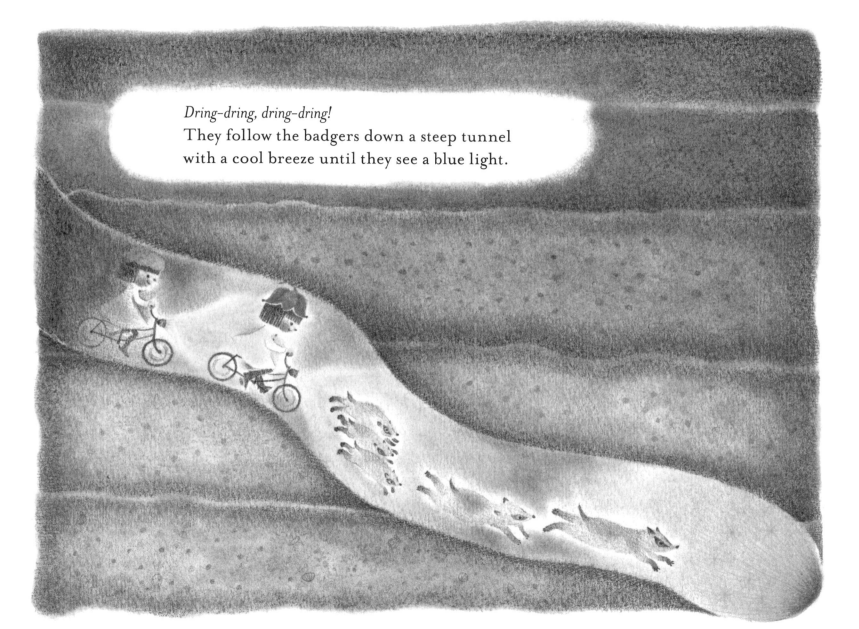

Dring-dring, dring-dring!
They follow the badgers down a steep tunnel
with a cool breeze until they see a blue light.

It's an underground lake with
little boats of all colors and shapes.

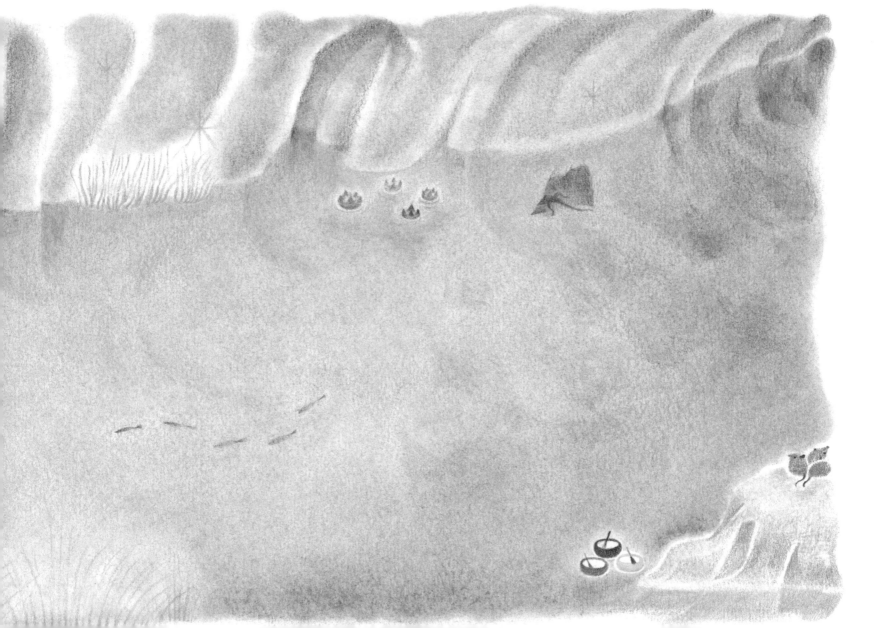

Dring-dring, dring-dring!
They hop aboard a boat and—

reach the other shore,
where the badgers make their home.

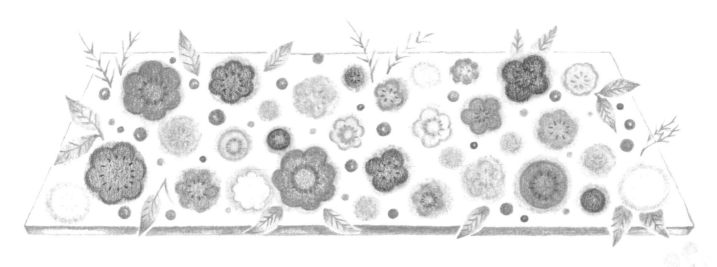

A beautiful meal awaits them—
a flowery arrangement of fried root vegetables
in all colors and shapes and bowls of blue soup
with beans in three colors.

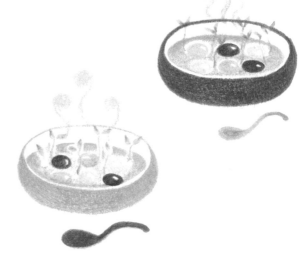

Chirri and Chirra eat their fill.

Then father badger starts to dig.

How long has it been?
Chirri and Chirra are sound asleep
when they hear—

"Please follow me."

Dring–dring, dring–dring!
Now they follow a tunnel
dug just for them.

They see a pink light.

Dring-dring, dring-dring!
It's the start of a wonderful day.

The End

Born in Tokyo, Kaya Doi graduated with a degree in design from Tokyo Zokei University.
She got her start in picture books by attending the Atosaki Juku Workshop, a program at a Tokyo bookshop.
Prolific and popular, Doi has created many wonderful books. She now lives in Chiba Prefecture
and maintains a strong interest in environmental and animal welfare issues.

David Boyd is Assistant Professor of Japanese at the University of North Carolina at Charlotte.
His translations have appeared in *Monkey Business International*, *Granta*, and *Words Without Borders*,
among other publications.

www.enchantedlion.com

First edition, published in 2019 by Enchanted Lion Books,
67 West Street, 317A, Brooklyn, NY 11222
Text and illustrations copyright © 2013 by Kaya Doi
English translation rights arranged with Alicekan Ltd. through Japan UNI Agency, Inc.
All rights reserved under International and Pan-American Copyright Conventions.
A CIP record is on file with the Library of Congress. ISBN 978-1-59270-224-2
Printed in China in January 2019 by RR Donnelley Asia Printing Solutions Ltd.
1 3 5 7 9 10 8 6 4 2

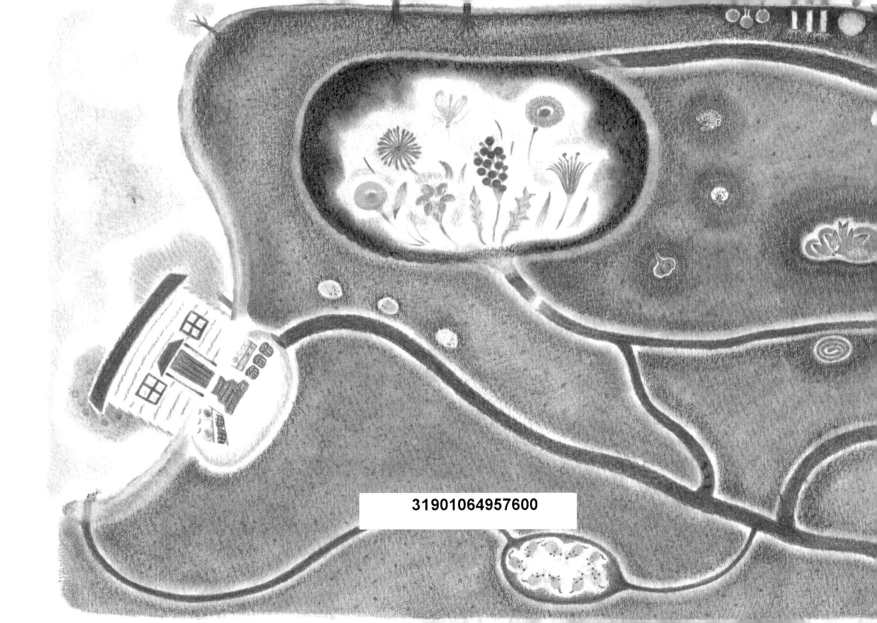

31901064957600